Engine Stories

EGMONT
We bring stories to life

First published in Great Britain in 2013 by Dean,
an imprint of Egmont UK Limited
The Yellow Building, 1 Nicholas Road, London W11 4AN

HiT entertainment

Thomas the Tank Engine & Friends™

CREATED BY BRITT ALLCROFT
Based on the Railway Series by the Reverend W Awdry
© 2013 Gullane (Thomas) LLC. A HIT Entertainment company.
Thomas the Tank Engine & Friends and Thomas & Friends are trademarks of Gullane (Thomas) Limited.
Thomas the Tank Engine & Friends and Design is Reg. U.S. Pat. & Tm. Off.

ISBN 978 0 6035 6799 5
54123/1
Printed in China

Engine Stories

This book belongs to:

....

Contents

Meet the Engines

Thomas

Rheneas

Rusty

Peter Sam

Gordon

Donald

Sir Handel

Douglas

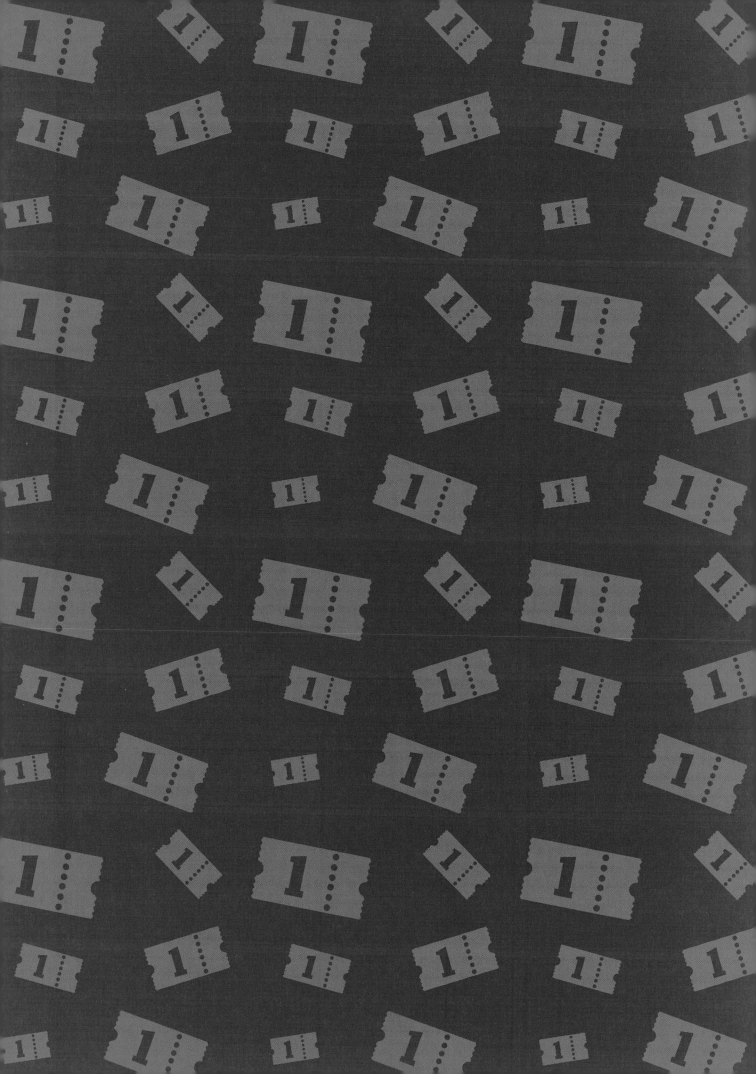

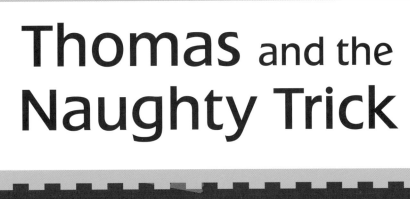

Thomas and the Naughty Trick

One day, Thomas was fitted with a brand new whistle.

The whistle gleamed . . . and Thomas beamed!

He blew his new whistle all day long.

He blew it softly . . . and he blew it LOUDLY!

Thomas blew his new whistle in stations . . . and in Misty Valley.

Thomas thought it was the most wonderful whistle he'd ever had.

Thomas puffed into the Wharf, pulling a train of empty trucks behind him.

The Thin Controller was there to greet him.

"Thomas," said The Thin Controller, "the narrow gauge engines are bringing bricks, flour and timber."

He told Thomas that the bricks, flour and timber had to be loaded into his trucks by teatime.

Then The Thin Controller left.

Thomas was very happy to have such a special job and he blew his new whistle loudly.

Rheneas was so surprised that he JUMPED – and the pipes all fell off his trucks.

Thomas thought it was very funny!

"That was fun!" he tooted.

Thomas wanted to play more jokes on his friends.

Later that day, Rusty puffed into the Wharf, shunting trucks full of red bricks. The bricks were to be unloaded into Thomas' trucks.

Thomas rolled up behind Rusty.

The little engines held their puff as Thomas blew his new whistle. "PEEP!"

Rusty JUMPED – and biffed into his trucks. Suddenly, he was covered in red brick dust!

The little engines all laughed at poor Rusty.

Thomas thought it was tremendous fun!

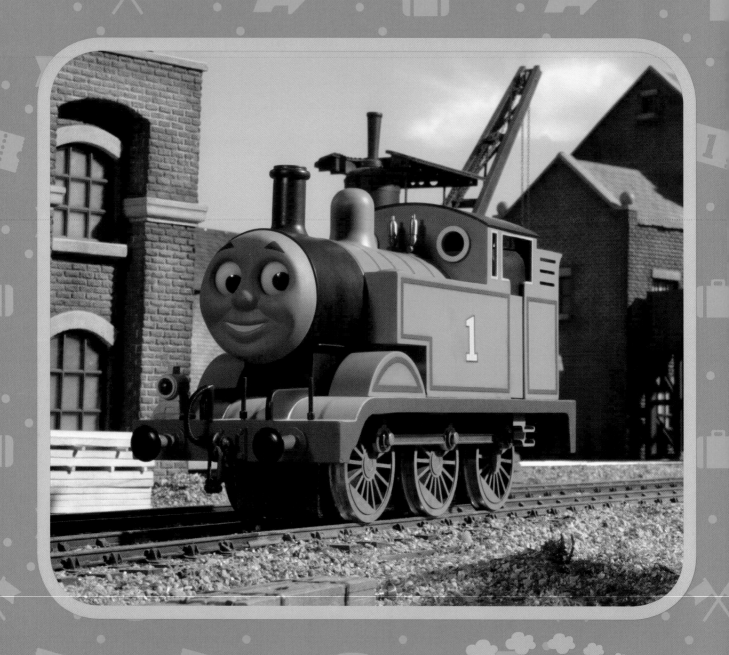

Rusty wanted to join in with all the fun the other engines were having.

"Can't catch me!" called Rusty, steaming around the Wharf.

Thomas puffed along beside him as everyone laughed.

They were all having so much fun . . . that they forgot about unloading the bricks!

Thomas had another idea.

"Sir Handel will be arriving with the trucks of flour soon," he tooted. "Why don't we all 'peep' him at once?"

The little engines thought it was a very exciting idea. They all found hiding places in the warehouse.

When Sir Handel puffed into the Wharf, there was nobody to be seen!

"Now!" Thomas cried, and he blew his new whistle as loudly as he could.

From their hiding places, the little engines blew their whistles, too!

"PEEP! PEEP!"

Sir Handel biffed his trucks in surprise – making flour fly up into the air like a great white cloud!

"You look like a ghost!" laughed Rusty.

Sir Handel thought it was very funny indeed.

"Woo!" he laughed. "Look at me – I'm a ghost!"

And he steamed away.

Soon, all the engines were chasing each other . . . and still no one was loading up Thomas' trucks with bricks!

Thomas had another idea.

"Peter Sam is on his way," tooted Thomas. "Let's 'peep' him as well!"

The little engines agreed this was a very good idea.

As Peter Sam trundled into the Wharf, Thomas got ready with his whistle . . .

The little engines got their whistles ready, too.

"PEEP!" went Thomas and the little engines.

Peter Sam shot forwards and bashed into his flatbeds, which were stacked with timber.

They burst through the buffers, smashed through a pile of oil drums . . .

. . . and SPLASHED straight into the canal!

"Oh my!" cried the little engines.

"Cinders and ashes!" gasped Thomas.

The Thin Controller arrived at the Wharf.

"What has been going on here?" he said, angrily. "There are bricks on the rails, there's flour all over the warehouse and timber in the canal!"

Thomas rolled forwards, looking guilty.

"I'm sorry, Sir," he wheeshed, sadly. "It's all my fault. I just wanted to play tricks and have some fun."

The Thin Controller was very cross.

"You must clear up this mess at once!" he cried. "And your trucks must be loaded by teatime."

Later on that day, The Thin Controller came back to check on the engines.

He saw Thomas looking pleased with himself. But he couldn't see Thomas' trucks!

"Where are your trucks?" asked The Thin Controller, very crossly.

Thomas smiled to himself. He was playing another naughty trick!

He puffed forwards slowly so The Thin Controller could see the trucks, which were full of bricks, flour and timber. Thomas had been hiding them as a joke!

"Here they are, Sir!" he whistled, happily. "Loaded up and ready to go!"

The little engines laughed.

Soon, The Thin Controller was laughing, too. "That was a funny joke, Thomas!" he said. "You are a Really Funny Engine!"

Thomas and the Naughty Trick Story Quiz

Question 1: What was Thomas fitted with?

    a) a new whistle

    b) a fog light

    c) new cowcatchers

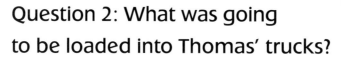

Question 2: What was going to be loaded into Thomas' trucks?

    a) passengers

    b) coal

    c) bricks, flour and timber

Question 3: Who did Thomas first make jump?

    a) Percy

    b) Edward

    c) Rheneas

Question 4: Who was shunting trucks full of red bricks?

    a) Diesel

    b) Rusty

    c) James

Question 5: What did Sir Handel arrive with?
- a) flowers
- b) trucks of flour
- c) passengers

Question 6: Who was covered in flour?
- a) Sir Handel
- b) Thomas
- c) Rusty

Question 7: Which engine knocked timber into the canal?
- a) Percy
- b) Emily
- c) Peter Sam

Question 8: Who was very cross?
- a) The Thin Controller
- b) The Fat Controller
- c) Lady Hatt

Answers on page 78

Gordon and the Engineer

Gordon and the Engineer

All the engines on the Island of Sodor have favourite jobs.

Gordon loves to pull the Express. He thinks it's the most important job on the Island.

And Gordon really likes to feel important!

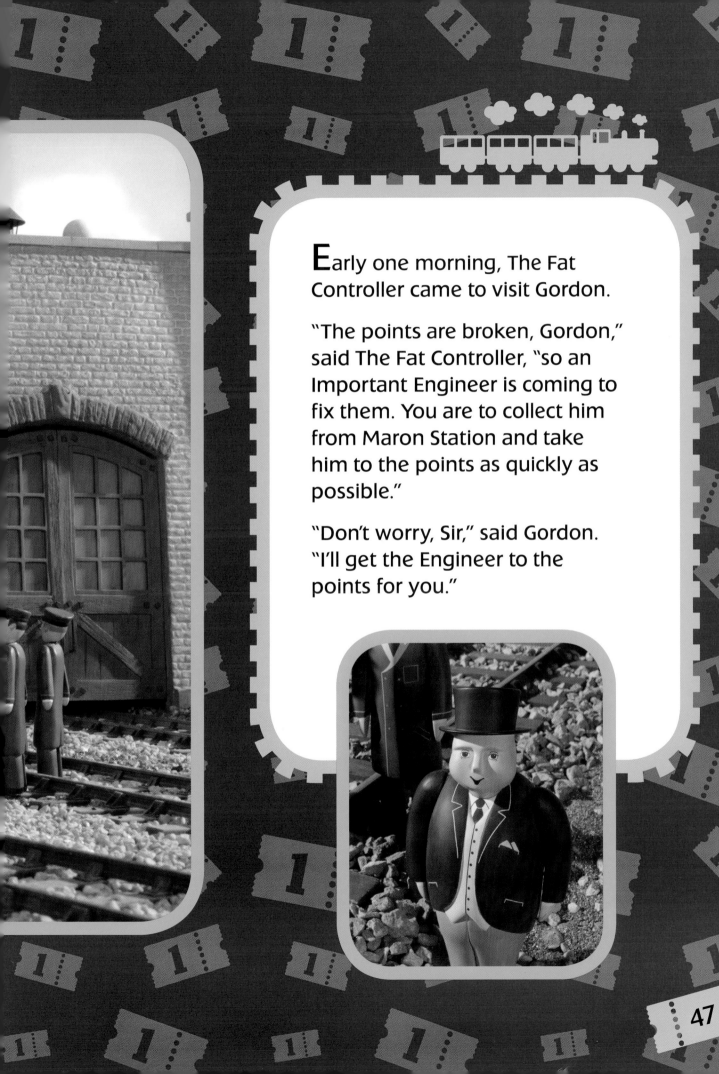

Early one morning, The Fat Controller came to visit Gordon.

"The points are broken, Gordon," said The Fat Controller, "so an Important Engineer is coming to fix them. You are to collect him from Maron Station and take him to the points as quickly as possible."

"Don't worry, Sir," said Gordon. "I'll get the Engineer to the points for you."

Gordon steamed off as fast as he could to Maron Station.

He was very proud to have been given such an important task.

"I'm an Important Engine collecting an Important Passenger," Gordon puffed, grandly.

He chuffed quickly past Henry. None of the other engines could go anywhere until the points were fixed.

Gordon pulled into Maron Station.

There was a passenger holding a toolbox waiting on the platform.

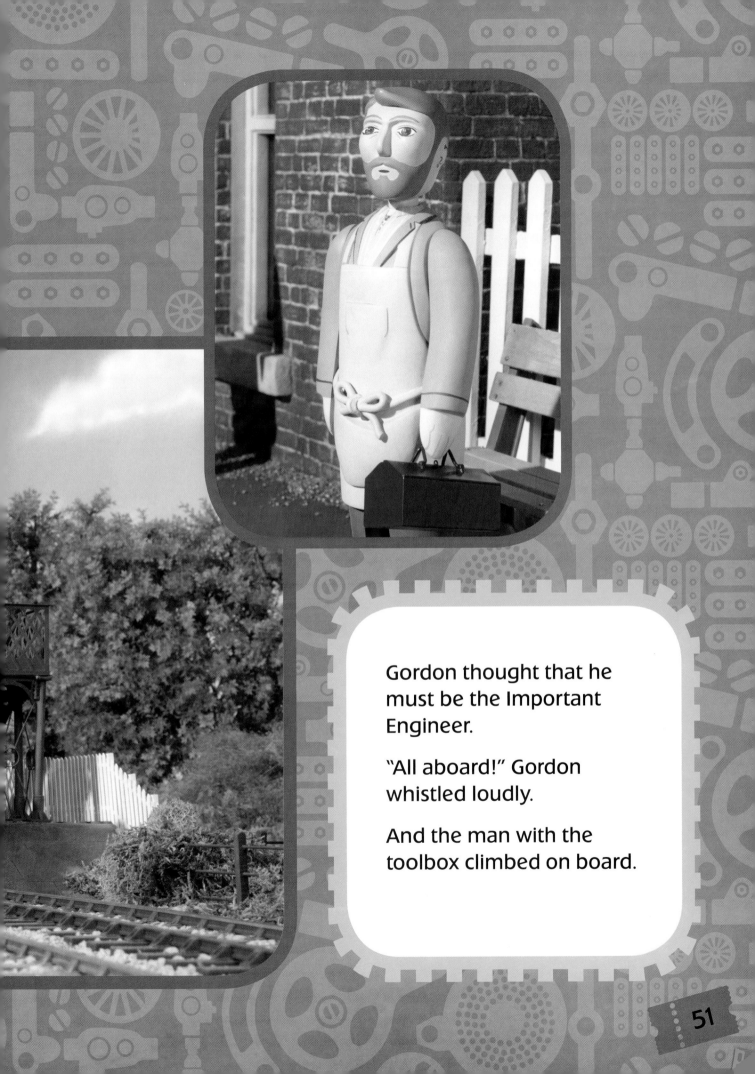

Gordon thought that he must be the Important Engineer.

"All aboard!" Gordon whistled loudly.

And the man with the toolbox climbed on board.

But as Gordon was getting ready to leave, the Stationmaster called to him.

"Wait!" shouted the Stationmaster. "You can't leave yet. Bertie the Bus is bringing more passengers!"

But Gordon told the Stationmaster he had to go.

"I can't wait!" he huffed. "I have a Very Important Passenger on board. I must leave now!"

And Gordon steamed away from the station.

Gordon puffed proudly through the countryside.

"I must get to the broken points, I must get to the broken points," he wheeshed.

But what Gordon didn't know was that the man with the toolbox wasn't the Engineer!

After Gordon had left Maron Station, Bertie the Bus had dropped the other passengers off – including the Engineer!

"Oh no, I've missed my train!" groaned the Engineer. "How will I fix the points now?"

Unaware of what had happened, Gordon continued steaming along the tracks.

He rattled past Donald then clattered past Douglas.

"Important engine coming through!" Gordon chuffed.

This made Douglas very annoyed!

Meanwhile, the man with the toolbox was very pleased. He was the only passenger and didn't have to stop at any of the stations.

Soon, Gordon arrived at the broken points. The man with the toolbox got out.

Thomas was waiting for them.

"I'm so glad you're here!" puffed Thomas. "None of the engines can move until the points are fixed!"

But the man with the toolbox was very confused.

"I'm not an Engineer!" the man said. "I am a carpenter. I thought Gordon was taking me to the Docks!"

Gordon realised his mistake – he'd picked up the wrong passenger! He quickly explained to the Signalman.

"I have to go back and get the Engineer," Gordon moaned.

"Sorry, Gordon," said the Signalman. "You can't reverse down the Express line with the Express."

Gordon was very worried. How were the points going to get fixed now?

Then Thomas had an idea.

"Why don't you go on my line?" chuffed Thomas, helpfully.

"That's a great idea!" puffed Gordon. "Thanks, Thomas."

Gordon left his coaches behind then steamed onto Thomas' track.

He reversed as quickly as he could down Thomas' line.

But soon he found Douglas blocking his route!

"Out of my way!" huffed Gordon. "I need to collect an Important Passenger!'

"But you can't get past," Douglas chuffed. "I can only go back as far as the next station, then Donald is in the way!"

Gordon felt terrible.

All the engines were stuck and it was all his fault.

"How am I going to collect the Engineer now?" he puffed sadly.

Suddenly, Gordon had an idea.

"Maybe all of the engines can help," he thought to himself.

Gordon told Douglas his plan.

"That's brilliant, Gordon!" peeped Douglas. "I'll go and tell Donald straight away."

Douglas puffed down the track to tell Donald about Gordon's idea.

"What a grand plan!" Donald whistled.

Then Donald steamed back to collect the Engineer from Maron Station.

The Engineer was very pleased to see Donald.

He climbed on board and Donald chuffed back up the line.

Donald dropped the Engineer off at the station for Douglas to pick him up.

With the Engineer on board, Douglas quickly steamed up the line.

Gordon was waiting at the next stop for Douglas and the Engineer to arrive.

Finally, Gordon picked up the Engineer. His plan had worked!

Gordon soon reached the broken points with the Engineer.

The Engineer fixed the points quickly, the engines could all chuff through happily.

Soon the railway was back to normal. Thomas was very proud of his friend.

"Your plan worked!" Thomas tooted. "Thank you, Gordon!"

"I couldn't have done it without your help, Thomas," puffed Gordon. "Even an Important Engine like me needs help . . . sometimes!"

Gordon and the Engineer Story Quiz

Question 1: Who asked Gordon to collect the Engineer?
   a) The Fat Controller
   b) The Thin Controller
   c) Thomas

Question 2: Where did Gordon pick up the wrong passenger from?
   a) the Docks
   b) Maron Station
   c) the Quarry

Question 3: Who did Gordon clatter past?
   a) Donald and Douglas
   b) Thomas
   c) Percy

Question 4: Who was waiting at the broken points?
   a) The Fat Controller
   b) Thomas
   c) Cranky

Question 5: What job did the man with the toolbox have?

    a) a carpenter

    b) a driver

    c) a guard

Question 6: Who was blocking Gordon's route?

    a) James

    b) Edward

    c) Douglas

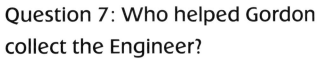

Question 7: Who helped Gordon collect the Engineer?

    a) Donald and Douglas

    b) Emily

    c) Percy

Question 8: Who fixed the points?

    a) The Fat Controller

    b) Thomas

    c) the Engineer

Answers on page 79

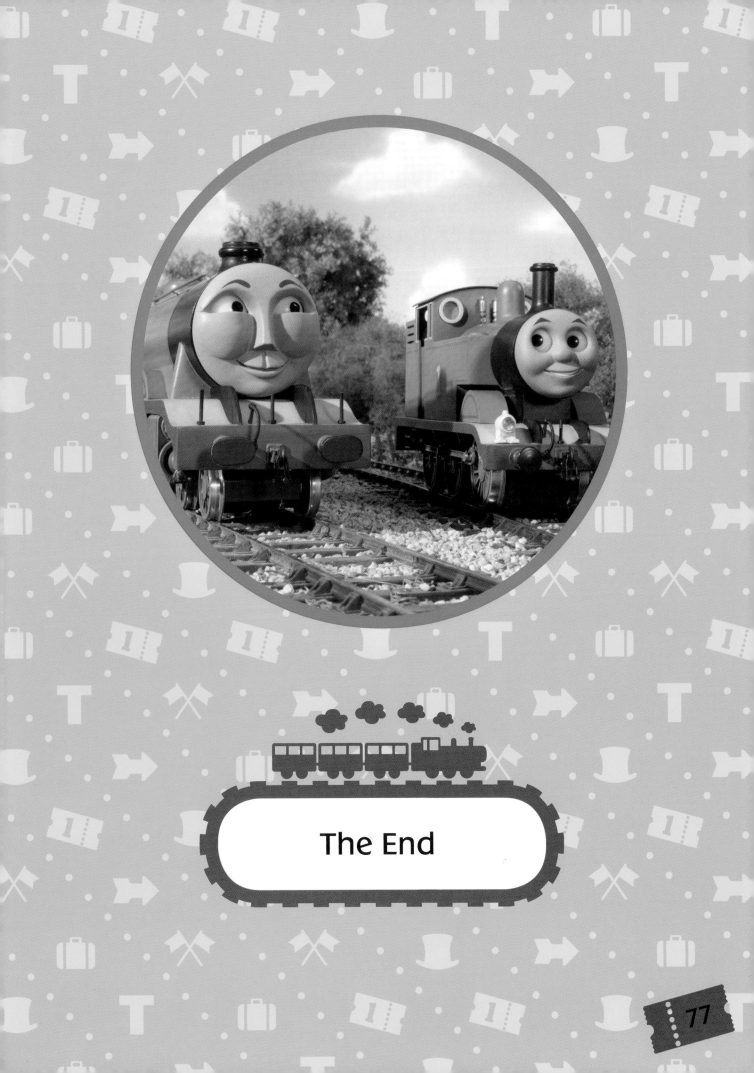

The End

Thomas and the Naughty Trick Story Quiz

Question 1: a) a new whistle

Question 2: c) bricks, flour and timber

Question 3: c) Rheneas

Question 4: b) Rusty

Question 5: b) trucks of flour

Question 6: a) Sir Handel

Question 7: c) Peter Sam

Question 8: a) The Thin Controller

Gordon and the Engineer Story Quiz

Question 1: a) The Fat Controller

Question 2: b) Maron Station

Question 3: a) Donald and Douglas

Question 4: b) Thomas

Question 5: a) a carpenter

Question 6: c) Douglas

Question 7: a) Donald and Douglas

Question 8: c) the Engineer